D0690563

AMY WU
and the
PERFECT BAO

Not like "bow."*
BAO like "bow"!
*AUTHOR'S NOTE: Growing up in a Mandarin-speaking family, I always said "bao zi" instead of "bao," and pronounced the word differently. But the Americanized pronunciation is usually "bow."

 • ISBN 978-1-338-81434-7 • Published by Scholastic Inc., 557 Broadway, New York, NY 10012, by arrangement with Aladdin, an imprint of Simon & Schuster Children's Publishing Division.
12 11 10 9 8 7 6 5 4 22 23 24 25 26 • Printed in the U.S.A. 40
First Scholastic printing, October 2021 • Designed by Laura Lyn DiSiena • The illustrations for this book were rendered digitally. • The text of this book was set in Andes Rounded.

To Mom and Dad, who helped me make bao even when my hands were too small —K. Z.

For my Ah Koo and Ah Yee, who made many yummy treats for me when I was a kid —C. C.

AMY WU and the PERFECT BAO

By KAT ZHANG
Illustrated by CHARLENE CHUA

SCHOLASTIC INC.

Amy can do a lot of things.

She can brush her teeth.

She can tie her shoe.

She can even do both at
once . . . sort of.

But there's one thing Amy cannot,

cannot do. She cannot make

THE PERFECT BAO.

Sometimes they come out too small.

Sometimes they
come out too **big**.

Sometimes she adds **too much** filling.

Sometimes **not enough**.

And sometimes they **fall apart** before they reach her mouth.

Amy's mom and dad make **perfect bao**.

So does her grandma.

Their bao are soft and fluffy and so, so **delicious**.

Amy could eat them all day. (Sometimes she does.)

Today, Amy is going to do it—**she's going to make the world's most perfect bao**. Bao making is an all-day event.

Amy's dad starts in the morning, mixing together the ingredients for the dough.

Then it's time to knead, knead, knead.
He pushes the dough! He punches
the dough!

Amy gives it a try too.

They leave the dough to rise. Amy keeps an eye on it, just in case. It grows bigger . . . and bigger . . . and even **bigger**.

Amy's dad squishes the dough down just in time.

He rolls it into a log and cuts it into pieces.

Meanwhile, Amy's mom
seasons meat for the filling.

Everyone gathers around the
table and rolls up their sleeves.
It's time to get to work!

Amy's first bao turns out a little funny. So does the second.

It's hard to know how much filling to add. Too little and the bao is sad and empty. Too much and—**oops**!

It’s also hard to pinch
the bao shut just right.
PINCH
PINCH
PINCH

Amy watches her mom
make a **perfect bao**.

She watches her dad
make a **perfect bao**—

and her grandma, too.

They all try to teach her.

"Roll out the dough like this," says Amy's dad.

"Use just enough filling," says Amy's mom.

"Pinch, pinch, pinch!" says Amy's grandma.

But Amy's bao just aren't the same.
They are too empty
or too fat.
They have holes in them.
They leak.

Maybe today won't be the day after all.

Maybe Amy just can't make a **perfect bao**.

Then Amy has an **idea.**

The pieces of dough were cut for grown-up hands. But Amy's hands are very small.

She whispers her idea into her grandma's ear.

Amy's grandma cuts each piece of dough into two smaller pieces. **Amy-size pieces**.

Now they fit perfectly in Amy's palms.

Carefully Amy rolls the dough
so it's thicker on the inside
and thinner at the edges.

She adds just the right amount of filling.

She
PINCH, PINCH, PINCHES
it shut.

And there it is!

AMY'S PERFECT BAO!

She makes another. And another. And even more after that.

She's a bao-making **MASTER**!

Soon all the dough and filling are gone.
Everyone is tired, but they're not done yet.
Amy's grandma boils a big pot of water.
It's time to steam the bao.

Amy keeps an eye on the steamer, just in case. All her perfect bao—and all the imperfect ones too—are snug inside.

The bao are done!
Amy's mom lifts the lid
off the steamer.

WHOOSH!

Out comes a puff of steam.
Amy can't see anything at all.

The steam clears.

There are Amy's **perfect bao**. They are not too small. They are not too big.

They have just the right amount of filling, and they do not leak.

They are soft and fluffy and so, so **delicious**.

Amy eats one, then another.
Then she eats one of
the **not-so-perfect bao**.
And you know what?
It tastes just as good.

EXIT
BAO
BAO

AMY'S FAMILY RECIPE (makes 20 bao)

Be sure to ask for help from a trusted grown-up when preparing this recipe. Have fun!

BAO DOUGH

1 packet active dry yeast (2¼ tsp.)
½ cup warm water
4 cups all-purpose flour
2 tsp. baking powder
2 tsp. salt
¼ cup sugar
1 cup low-fat milk
2 tbsp. vegetable oil

BAO DOUGH INSTRUCTIONS

1. Add the yeast to the ½ cup of warm water along with a large pinch of the sugar, and mix until the yeast dissolves. The water should turn frothy in a few minutes.
2. In a large bowl, combine 3½ cups flour, baking powder, salt, and the rest of the sugar. Mix together.
3. Add the milk, oil, and yeast-water to the dry ingredients. Mix together until the wet and dry ingredients are incorporated, then knead 5–10 minutes until the dough is soft and elastic. Slowly add the remaining ½ cup of flour as needed. When the dough has been sufficiently kneaded, a thumbprint pressed into the dough should slowly spring back.
4. Form the dough into a ball and place it back into the large bowl. Cover the bowl with plastic wrap and leave it in a warm place for 1–1½ hours until the dough has doubled in size.
5. Gently punch down the dough and knead it for another 5 minutes. Place it back into the bowl, cover it with the plastic wrap, and leave it to rise for another hour.

BAO FILLING

½ lb. raw shrimp (no shells or tails)
½ lb. raw ground pork
1 egg
2 tbsp. rice wine
1 tsp. sesame oil
2 tbsp. soy sauce
2 tbsp. fish sauce
Pinch of pepper
1 tsp. ginger powder
5 shiitake mushrooms, minced
3 cloves garlic, minced
2 tsp. fresh ginger, minced
Salt to taste

BAO FILLING INSTRUCTIONS

1. Dice the shrimp into small pieces and add to the ground pork, egg, rice wine, sesame oil, soy sauce, fish sauce, pepper, and ginger powder in a large bowl.
2. Add the minced shiitake mushrooms, garlic, and ginger to the bowl. Mix all the ingredients to combine, but do not overmix.
3. A spoonful of the mixture can be cooked like a meatball in boiling water or fried in a pan to allow for tasting. If needed, add additional salt.

BAO-MAKING INSTRUCTIONS

1. Cut 20 2-inch squares of parchment paper.
2. Shape the bao dough into a rough log approximately 3 inches in diameter, and cut 20 pieces of equal size.
3. Take a piece of dough and flatten it into a rough circle by hand or with a rolling pin. The circle should be approximately 4 inches in diameter, and thicker at the center than at the edges.
4. Place about a tablespoonful of bao filling into the center of the dough circle. It is better to start with smaller amounts of filling, to make the pleating easier. Pleat the bao shut by pinching the edges of the dough circle until the top comes together like a drawstring purse. There are many videos online that show the pleating process!
5. Place each pleated bao on a square of parchment paper.
6. Pleated bao should sit for about 15 minutes before being steamed. Generally it takes at least this long to pleat all the bao, so by the time you are finished pleating all 20, the first few will be ready to go in the steamer.
7. Steam the bao, with the parchment paper underneath, in a steamer for 10 minutes. Remove the steamer from the heat for 3–4 minutes before removing the lid, to keep the bao from deflating.
8. Eat!

Photo by Alice Hong

KAT ZHANG loves traveling to places both real and fictional. The former have better souvenirs, but the latter allow for dragons, so it's a tough choice. A writer of books for teens and children, she spends her free time scribbling poetry, taking photographs, and climbing atop things she shouldn't.

Photo by Wayne Santos

CHARLENE CHUA draws many things, from bao to dragons to (literally) the kitchen sink. When she is not drawing, she enjoys playing with or talking to her cats. (They listen politely—most of the time.) Charlene grew up in Singapore and now lives in Canada. Her favorite bao are char siu bao!